Lucky

LUCKY

Little Guy,
BIG Mission!

by Eileen Doyon with
Christy Gardner

Illustrated by
Susan Spellman

Published by Piscataqua Press
32 Daniel St., Portsmouth NH 03801
www.ppressbooks.com
info@piscataquapress.com

ISBN: 978-1-950381-39-5

Printed in the United States of America

50% of profits from Lucky...Little Guy, BIG Mission will go to Christy Gardner. Christy will be using a percentage for her charity organization for training service dogs, helping Veterans, and promoting Sled Hockey.

**Thank you so much for your support in her mission.
Tell your friends...and the book makes a great gift.
Remember, we love reviews!**

This book is dedicated to Christy Gardner.

I first met Christy in 2014 when she wrote a story about Moxie, her service dog, in my book, *Pet Tales*.

She inspired me from the moment I met her. First, thank you for your service to our great country. Christy is an Army Veteran. After being injured in the line of duty and after overcoming extraordinary physical, mental, and emotional issues, Christy tackles life each and every day with 150% effort and never gives up! She is such an inspiration to all as she lives life, plays Sled Hockey and competes in other sports all around the globe.

With Moxie by her side, she now is training other puppies, like Lucky, to become service/therapy dogs to help other Veterans.

Christy, you are an amazing Veteran, lady, and athlete. I am honored to know you as a person and proud to be your friend. This book is for YOU!

It's a beautiful day in New England and several people are coming to look at Lucy's puppies. They're all playing with each other...

...except for Tiny Tim.

Lucy explains to her puppies, "Someone will be taking each one of you home and will make you feel very special. You will become part of their family!"

Lucy notices that no one has been playing with Tiny Tim. He was born with a club front paw and runs hobbling with his leg.

Tiny Tim tells his mama, "No one wants me because of my funny paw. I am too different from the rest of my brothers and sisters."

Lucy hugs Tiny Tim. She tells him, "Someone very special will be here to give you a wonderful home. You wait and see."

Christy arrives the very next day with her dog Moxie. Moxie is wearing a special jacket that says "service dog."

Tiny Tim asks, "What does service dog mean mama?" Lucy explains to Tiny Tim that Moxie is very, very special. She helps Christy by guiding her and protecting her from harm's way.

Tiny Tim asks, "Was she born that way like me?"

Lucy says, "No, she served in the Army and was injured in the line of duty."

Tiny Tim runs right up to Moxie. He says, "Wow, I wish I could do what you do, and help people."

Christy and Moxie go over and start playing with Tiny Tim. They seem to be enjoying the play time. Tiny Tim is having so much fun playing with Moxie but knows that they will be leaving soon like all the others.

Christy walks over to Lucy and starts talking with her.

Lucy runs over to Tiny Tim and tells him, "Christy wants to take you home and teach you to be a service dog like Moxie."

Tiny Tim dances and runs and hobbles in circles. "They want ME, they want ME. Christy and Moxie want ME!"

Happy tears begin to fall from Tiny Tim's eyes.

Tiny Tim gathers his belongings and hobbles and runs over to his mama. He tells her, "I am so happy! I will miss you but will make you proud. I am going to be a "service dog" and help people just like Moxie!"

Lucy tells Tiny Tim, "I know you will be a great service dog for someone. You are very special. I love you."

"I love you too, Mama."

They arrive at Tiny Tim's new home. Christy shows him where he will be sleeping, right next to Moxie.

Tiny Tim says, "I am the luckiest puppy in the whole wide world!" Thank you, Christy and Moxie!"

Christy shouts, "That's it, we will call you Lucky!"

The sun is bright and shining the very next day. Christy, Moxie and Lucky head to the park to play. Lucky is so excited. He hobbles and runs around and sees other puppies to play with. They all look at Lucky and laugh at him.

"What are you doing here? You don't belong here. You can't play catch like us."

Lucky hangs his head down and turns around to walk away.

Moxie runs over to Lucky. The other puppies are watching. Moxie tells Lucky, "Come on Lucky, come play ball with me." The other puppies are surprised. They all look up to Moxie. Moxie shouts out, "Way to go Lucky!" as he catches the ball.

Lucky hobbles and runs over to the other puppies. He says to them, "Yes, I can play ball like all of you."

One of the puppies, Bully Bob goes up to Lucky. He says, "You think you can do everything we can do, well, you can't dig a hole, gimpy."

Lucky looks at Moxie.

Moxie says, "Oh yes he can. Lucky, turn around and start digging with your hind legs."

Lucky does what Moxie tells him to do and he kicks and kicks and digs a hole.

Lucky uses his front good paw to finish smoothing out the dirt.

Bully Bob walks up to Lucky. He says, "I guess you can do everything we can do. You are special. I am sorry I called you gimpy. That was wrong of me. Come and play with us."

Lucky hobbles and runs to play with all the other puppies.

Christy, Moxie and Lucky get into their van. Time to go home after playing all afternoon and making new friends. Lucky turns to Moxie, "Thank you for making me feel so very special."

Christy asks, "How about an ice cream and treats for each of you?"
Moxie and Lucky bark and give a wag of their tail. Christy tells
them, "Let's go to our favorite place, Lickee's & Chewy's!"

They enter Lickee's & Chewy's, The Kingdom of Caramelot. Lucky looks around at all the candy and sweets. He says, "Wow, this store is awesome. It has everything."

They each order an ice cream sundae with a biscuit treat on top. Christy buys some fudge and candy to take with her.

They return home. Lucky is tired. He turns to Christy and Moxie and says, "I love my new home, my new friends and my new family."

Christy says, "We love you too Lucky," and Moxie wags her tail.

Christy tells them, "It has been a long day. Time to get some sleep. Tomorrow there will be more adventures and more friends to meet. Remember Lucky, you are a little guy with a BIG mission ahead of you."

Moxie and Lucky are curled up in their beds. Christy smiles and turns the light off and says to herself, "We are all very lucky to have each other. I will take him to the veterinarian this week to have them look at his club paw and see how they can help him best. We all want Lucky to be a service/therapy dog!"

Til tomorrow……night night….

Christy did take Lucky to the veterinarian, and he had surgery when he was three months old. He had quite the journey full of fun adventures, TV news shows and was one of the stars of the play, "Annie." Lucky passed his therapy dog test. Christy and Moxie worked with him and had the help of Claire Parker, the school's administrative assistant. Lucky is now officially a "certified therapy dog" at Leeds Central School in Maine. This happened all leading up to his very first birthday!

He now lives with Claire and comes to school each day to be available for students who need a little comfort, who need to calm down, or who just love him and want to say, "Hi!" His bed is in the Main Office, and he greets everyone who comes to visit. It creates such a warm and welcoming environment and sets the tone for the positive and caring climate of their school.

A special "thank you" to Jennifer Groover who started it all by inviting Christy and Moxie to speak during an assembly and to Danielle Harris, the school's principal, for having the dream of getting a dog at her school for the children.

More stories of Lucky's journey and adventures to come…

Christy was injured in the Army in 2006. The doctors suggested a Service Dog might be of great benefit to her. Moxie is a trained seizure alert/response dog as well as a mobility assistance dog. Together, the two have helped raise and train ten puppies to become working service and therapy dogs. The story of Lucky Tim is that of puppy number ten, a special puppy with an incredible personality and a special mission.

On any given day in Lewiston, Maine, you can find Christy and Moxie walking the neighborhood together. They visit fellow Veterans at the local VA Hospital and Maine Veterans' Homes and help mentor others in need. Always up for a challenge, this dynamic duo has assisted others with disabilities to conquer their own obstacles by starting the New England Warriors Hockey Club for disabled Veterans along with volunteering on the board of Central Maine Adaptive Sports.

Outside of training puppies, Christy and Moxie train together for Team USA! Christy is in her eighth season on the US Women's Sled Hockey Team and is also training in hopes of making the US Track & Field Team for Tokyo 2020 as a thrower with Moxie by her side.

The Story of Lickee's & Chewy's Candies & Creamery

It was a few days after Christmas in 2008 and I was deployed to Bagram Air Base, Afghanistan when one of the guys I worked with spun around in his chair and looked over at a table covered in a huge pile of candies, chips, cookies etc. that had been sent in care packages from our families back home and exclaims "That's a lot of lickies and chewies!" to which I responded, "That's a lot of what?" and he went on to explain how it is an old military term used to refer to snacks, candy, or other small items that soldiers bring with them during field training. I told him right then and there that I was going to open a candy store with that name some day because I have always loved candy, I love the flavors, the colors, the idea of being able to try a little at a time and most of all, the way it makes people feel … happy.

As fate would have it, in 2014, a few months after retiring from the military, a small candy store in my town went up for sale and of course I bought it. I added hundreds of new products the first year and then I started making chocolates, caramels, marshmallow and other treats.

After about three years, I could not keep up with demand in the tiny 500 square feet shop and needed to expand so I started looking for a place to build a new much larger candy store. I needed a large space that had a bit of a castle look to it because a couple years earlier I had come up with the idea that Lickee and Chewy would actually be characters, Lickee, a knight and Chewy, a dragon and they would be from the Kingdom of Caramelot! Again fate stepped in and brought us to Dover, NH and the nearly 200 year old mills in the center of town where I was able to create Lickee's & Chewy's Candies & Creamery, a very unique chocolate, candy and ice cream kingdom with a medieval castle theme at the base of a "castle tower" that opened in September 2018.

Thus began the story of not only Lickee's & Chewy's the candy company, but even more importantly, so also began the Sweet Adventures of Lickee & Chewy, two friends looking to help people enjoy their lives and make them smile by sharing their love of all things sweet with the world.

We have now been open for just over a year and have welcomed guests from all over New England and around the country to our store to experience our giant ice cream creations, handmade caramels and chocolates, one-of-kind 8 ft wide "candy round table" and selection of candies from around the world. Each day Lickee's & Chewy's Candies & Creamery works to fulfill its mission:

"To sweeten people's lives with exceptional

confections, extraordinary customer service

and by sharing our love and knowledge of

chocolate and candy with all our guests"

Thank you to our friends and family for being Sponsors for *Lucky...Little Guy, BIG Mission!*

Anonymous – To the Glory of God
Jacqueline Ahlquist – In honor of our Service Men and Women
Jay and Rachel Bishop – In loving memory of Zoey
Mary Bunnell – In honor of all cancer survivors
Missy Burke
Tammy Chisholm – In memory of service dogs Murphy and Tucker
Abigail Colbeth, Ryan Brewer and Maverick the yellow lab
Steve and Norma Crowell - In memory of Molly
Janet Dermody
Aidan Robert and Brady Daniel Donbeck
Denise Dube
Jessica Carpentier - In loving memory of Brine
Austin and Mia Fisher
Sandy and Bill Fisher
Patti and Ernie Gagne
Tasha Gerken
Gia Gould - Gould's Goldens
Yvette Goulet – In memory of Gizzie
Beth and Cali Bear Grauer
The Groover Family
Ted and Eleanor Heidrich – In memory of their dog Peter
Patricia Hesse - In memory of Lady
Brenda Kirk - For grandsons – Mason and Wyatt Henderson

Thank you to our friends and family for being Sponsors for *Lucky…Little Guy, BIG Mission!*

Kaelin Lavoie
Jennifer Siller Lasry
Leeds Central School Parent Teacher Committee
Lickee's & Chewy's Candies & Creamery
Maine Family Federal Credit Union
Rebecca Mann – In honor of Sully
Jay Marquiss
Sue Mills and my grandkids Lili and Luke
Claire Parker
Nochole Pingel
Karen, Matthew, Mackenzie and Dominique Richard - In memory of Spike #tripawdsrule
Cheryl Robert – In honor of Romeo
Emily, Lance and Brooke Robinson – In memory of Gunner and Titus
Susan Rooks
Richard and Corinne Ryan II
Karen Smith - In memory of Ginger
Zenita Smith – In honor of the amazing students at Richland R1, Essex, MO
Patty and Mitch Suprenant and their grandkids – Ellery, Gavin, Logan, Morgan, Kylie, Alita and Emma
Joanne Trust – In honor of Riley and KC
Richard L. Zeff Plastic Surgery
Debbie Zimmermann

About the Author

Eileen has released eight books in her series, Unforgettable Faces and Stories: *Dedications: Dads and Daughters/2013, Keepsakes: Treasures from the Heart/2013, Best Friends: Forever and Ever/2013, Pet Tales: Unconditional Love/2014* listed on Amazons Best Sellers list, *Letters To Heaven/2015,* also listed on Amazons Best Sellers list, *The Second My Life Changed Forever/2016, Starting Over, Stories of New Beginnings/2017,* and *Patriots of Courage, Tributes to First Responders/2018.*

Please visit her website www.UnforgettableFacesandStories.com and join her Facebook page, Unforgettable Faces And Stories https://www.facebook.com/unforgettablefacesandstories/ Follow her on Twitter @FacesandStories and Instagram @Eileen Doyon Unforgettable Faces & Stories. Her series was created after her dads' death in 2011 from lung cancer.

Eileen grew up in the small town of Fort Edward in upstate New York. She left there in 1978 and now lives in Portsmouth, New Hampshire with her husband, Dan and cat, Otis. She enjoys gardening and visiting new places, and familiar places, and meeting new friends. Dan and Eileen are members of Pease Greeters in Portsmouth

Eileen's mission is to help Christy train service dogs to help other Veterans and to train dogs to work in the classrooms with kids. The books will talk about anti-bullying, disabilities, and to never give up no matter what your situation.

Thank you to all our Veterans and First Responders.

About the Illustrator

Susan Spellman started her art career as a staff illustrator at a filmstrip company in Westport CT after getting a BA in art from Marymount College in Tarrytown, NY. She then began a career as a illustrator of children's books and magazines, and has illustrated more than 30 books to date. Recently, three of the books she has illustrated have won four national and regional awards. While continuing to work in illustration as a career, Susan has also increasingly focused on her interest in fine arts, exhibiting paintings in numerous regional galleries and art organizations throughout the North Shore.

She is an avid "Plein Air" painter, a portrait artist, and has been creating a collection of paintings of dancers,which has been on exhibition at the Massachusetts General Hospital Illuminations Program.

Susan is an art instructor at the Newburyport Art Association (NAA) specializing in drawing and portraiture, and a visiting artist to schools and art organizations throughout New England.

She is a member of the"Newburyport 10 Plein Air Painters" and has been a member of the Newburyport Art Association since 1996. She has a studio in Newburyport where she lives with her husband Jay McGovern.

More information can be found on her web site at

www.spelllmancollection.com

Thank you Christy and Moxie for taking me into your home!

Happy Trails...

Moxie